Colusa County Free Library
3 0738 00094 175 6

D0053699

Colusa County Free Library
738 Market Street
Colusa, CA 95932
Phone: 458-7671

CUP

a boy, a dog and a frog

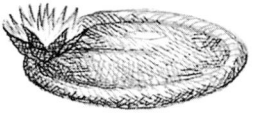

by mercer mayer

dial books for young readers
new  york

COLUSA COUNTY LIBRARY

To my family,
Marianna and Samantha

Published by Dial Books for Young Readers
A division of Penguin Putnam Inc.
345 Hudson Street
New York, New York 10014

Copyright © 1967 by Mercer Mayer
All rights reserved
ISBN 0-8037-2880-8
Library of Congress Catalog Card Number: 67-22254
Manufactured in China on acid-free paper

1 3 5 7 9 10 8 6 4 2